Two in One

BARON BEEFBURGER

and

DESMOND THE DRAGON

ILLUSTRATED BY JENNY PRESS

P · PARRAGON ·

This is a Parragon Book

©Parragon 1997

Parragon
13-17 Avonbridge Trading Estate
Atlantic Road, Avonmouth
Bristol. BS11 9QD

Produced by The Templar Company plc,
Pippbrook Mill, London Road, Dorking,
Surrey RH4 1JE

Designed by Janie Louise Hunt
Edited by Caroline Steeden
Printed and bound in Italy
ISBN 0 75252 506 9

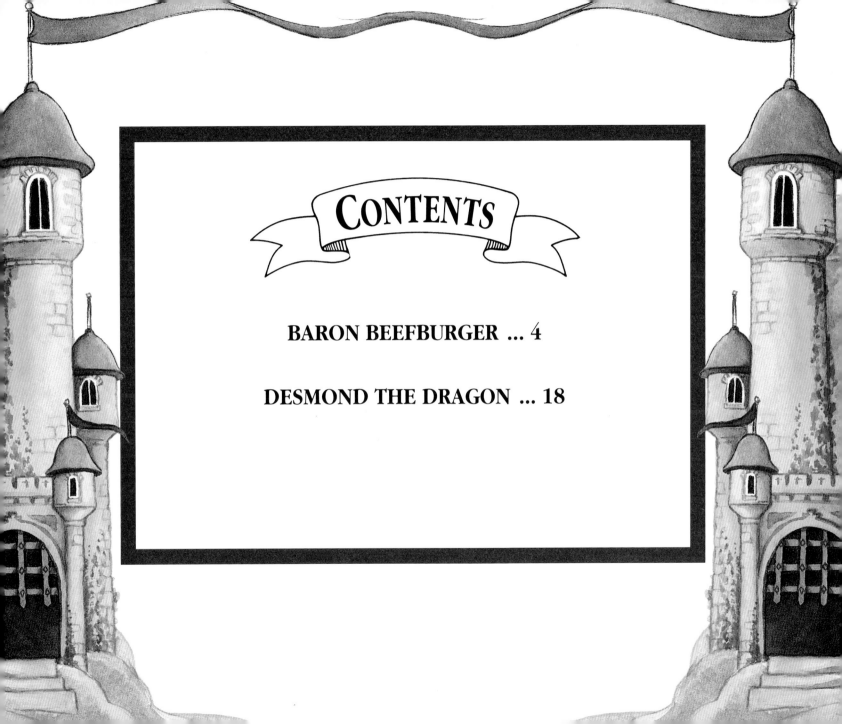

CONTENTS

BARON BEEFBURGER

WRITTEN BY CANDY WALLACE

A very long time ago in a far off land, lived the evil Baron Beefburger. He had a twirly black moustache and a silly haircut that looked as though someone had put a pudding basin on his head and cut round it. He dressed in black and always had an evil sneer on his face.

The baron lived in a great castle and made his courtiers' lives an absolute misery. Not only was he always grumpy, but there was nothing he liked better than to hurl a custard pie in someone's face.

The castle cooks worked day and night cooking the Baron's favourite beefburgers and an endless supply of custard pies, while the castle laundry worked overtime cleaning all the custardy clothes.

In the castle lived the beautiful Princess Petunia and a knight called Sir Fightalot. Sir Fightalot was madly in love with the princess and she rather liked him too. But the evil baron wanted the princess for himself. So poor Sir Fightalot received more than his fair share of custard pies and never had a clean suit of armour to wear.

One day, while Sir Fightalot was out jousting, the baron went to see the princess. When she saw him coming she put a box over her head quickly in case he had a custard pie with him.

"Come, come, my dear," said the baron in an oily voice. "I only want to talk to you." The princess took the box off her head and sat down with her chin in her hands looking glum. "What do you want?" she said, sulkily.

"I'm having a little dinner party tomorrow evening…" he said. 'Just for two…" and he put his face close to hers with a horrible smile. "I'd advise you to come, or you might find a custard pie in your bed…"

When Sir Fightalot returned and found out what the baron had been up to, he was hopping mad. Something had to be done. He decided to go and see his wise and tubby friend, Friar Tuckshop.

"We've got to do something about him," said Sir Fightalot to his friend the friar. "He's after the princess and everyone in the castle is sick and tired of being covered in custard."

Friar Tuckshop looked thoughtful. "There's only one creature in the land more powerful than the baron," he said finally. "About 20 leagues away from here lives a dragon in a cave on a hillside. He's the only available monster for miles. What's more, he's not too keen on the baron. I remember a couple of years ago the baron sent the entire army to kill the dragon and make him into an umbrella stand for the Great Hall. They didn't succeed, of course, but it didn't make a very good impression on the dragon. I think he might help us."

The next morning, they set off to find the dragon. Sir Fightalot's knees were knocking the whole way and Friar

Tuckshop had to stop every now and then for a restoring snack. After some hours, walking over hill and dale, they arrived at the dragon's cave. It was set halfway up a sheer rock face and they could see the smoke from the dragon's nostrils curling up into the air outside the cave. Sir Fightalot looked at Friar Tuckshop and gulped.

"Are you sure he won't eat us?" he said.

"No, I'm not," Friar Tuckshop replied, "but it's too late to go back now!"

The two intrepid but trembling travellers climbed up to the mouth of the cave and peered in.

"Good afternoon," said the dragon. "Would you care for a cup of tea?"

Now it's a funny thing about dragons. People are very scared of them and run away. When they do go near one it's usually because they want to kill it and take it back to impress some princess or other, which means that dragons get rather lonely and fed up.

So the dragon was really pleased to see the nervous, but friendly, Sir Fightalot and Friar Tuckshop. They found themselves being entertained to a pot of tea and a plate of fairy cakes. Very relieved they hadn't been eaten after all, they explained (in between mouthfuls of cake) about the troublesome baron's latest tricks. Together with the dragon (whose name was Humphrey) they devised a clever plan...

That night, the baron sat at one end of his huge dinner table in the Great Hall and poor Princess Petunia sat at the other end looking bored. The baron, with a napkin around his neck, was tucking into a plate of his favourite beefburgers smothered in tomato sauce. A pile of custard pies lay on the table ready for anyone who dared to interrupt his romantic candlelit dinner with the princess.

13

"Bah!" he spluttered, suddenly. "These beefburgers are burnt!" He turned in fury to a trembling footman. "Bring the cook to me this minute!" and he threw a custard pie at the poor man as he sped out of the door.

.Before you could say "knife and fork", the door to the Great Hall opened and in came — Humphrey the dragon! He was wearing a chef's hat and apron and wielding a giant wooden spoon. The baron was somewhat taken aback, but managed to shout:

"These beefburgers are burnt — you're fired!"

"No," replied the dragon. "You're fired," and he breathed on the baron's beefburgers. In seconds they were reduced to smouldering cinders. The princess began to think this wasn't going to be such a bad evening after all. The baron, meanwhile, was speechless with terror and held his napkin over his face.

Into the room came Sir Fightalot and Friar Tuckshop.

"Our friend Humphrey here is going to be the new cook," said Sir Fightalot to the baron. "If you ever pester Princess Petunia again, or throw another custard pie, he'll burn your beefburgers to a cinder. Is that clear?"

Princess Petunia gazed at Sir Fightalot and sighed. What a hero!

The baron spluttered and choked and went bright red and then deep purple. But he knew that he was beaten. What could a grumpy baron do against a big fire-breathing dragon?

After that, life was a lot easier at the castle.

Occasionally the baron just couldn't resist throwing a custard pie at someone and the dragon would burn his beefburgers that night. That would teach the baron a lesson — for a while, at least!

The princess was so impressed with brave Sir Fightalot that she married him.

Meanwhile, Humphrey the dragon stayed on as the castle cook and was very happy. He loved cooking and, best of all, he wasn't lonely any more. He never did go back to his cave on the hillside. To thank him for taming the baron, the courtiers gave him a whole tower to himself and the run of the castle kitchen. Everyone agreed he made the best fairy cakes they had ever eaten and his fiery barbecues were the talk of the land. And if the baron fancied a custard pie — he had to make it himself!

DESMOND THE DRAGON

WRITTEN BY AMBER HUNT

Young Desmond the Dragon was by now absolutely, utterly, and almost nearly sure that he wasn't a dragon. Oh, he was a respectable size, and growing all the time, and he was covered from ears to tail with very tough and very green scales. He had a forked tongue, just like all his friends, and four sets of fine claws as well as a good loud dragon-type roar. Desmond had to admit that he did look a lot like his mum and dad, but, despite all this, Desmond was still worried that he might not be a real dragon.

Each morning he looked in the mirror, twisting around to examine his back and each morning he saw — nothing. Dragons had wings, didn't they? If he was a dragon, where were his wings?

Then, after he had looked in the mirror, Desmond would go outside the cave into the garden and breathe out hard. Nothing. Dragons breathed fire, didn't they? If he was a dragon, where was his fire?

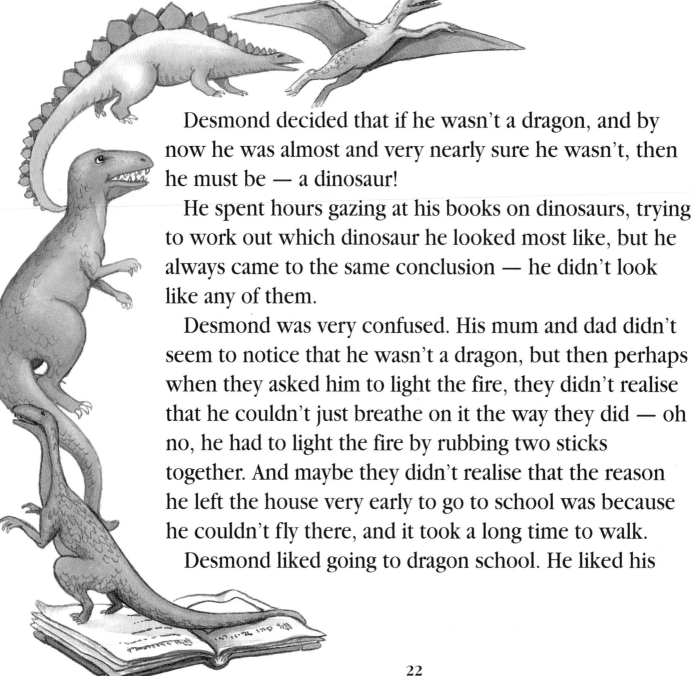

Desmond decided that if he wasn't a dragon, and by now he was almost and very nearly sure he wasn't, then he must be — a dinosaur!

He spent hours gazing at his books on dinosaurs, trying to work out which dinosaur he looked most like, but he always came to the same conclusion — he didn't look like any of them.

Desmond was very confused. His mum and dad didn't seem to notice that he wasn't a dragon, but then perhaps when they asked him to light the fire, they didn't realise that he couldn't just breathe on it the way they did — oh no, he had to light the fire by rubbing two sticks together. And maybe they didn't realise that the reason he left the house very early to go to school was because he couldn't fly there, and it took a long time to walk.

Desmond liked going to dragon school. He liked his

teachers and he had lots of friends, none of whom seemed to notice that he wasn't really a dragon. But then you weren't allowed to fly during school, so perhaps that was why they hadn't realised. The fact that he couldn't breathe fire wasn't a problem either; all dragons, upon arriving at school, had to drink a gallon of water. This prevented young dragons, who weren't yet properly fire-trained, from accidentally breathing out flames and setting fire to the school. So Desmond's secret was safe, for now.

Then one day Desmond woke up with a fang-ache. At first he wasn't sure what it was. He thought perhaps his head was lying on something sharp, but when he sat up the pain went with him and it followed him out of bed and all the way over to the mirror.

He looked in the mirror and didn't see himself looking back. Well, not the himself he was used to seeing.

The dragon, or possibly not dragon, he was looking at, had a huge swelling on the side of its face.

Desmond rushed downstairs to his mum.

"Mum," he mumbled, "look at my face. It has gone all lumpy and bumpy."

Desmond's mum looked at his face and, trying not to laugh, said, "Oh dear, I think you have been eating too many chocolate-covered bones. We'd better go and see Morris the Magician. He's a wonderful fangtist, amongst other things." She winked at Desmond's dad, and while Desmond went to get his hat, said to him, "I think it's time to get a couple of other things sorted out too while we're there, don't you, dear?"

So off they went to see Morris. "It's such a nice day," said Mrs Dragon, with a knowing smile. "I think we'll walk." And they did, much to Desmond's relief.

Desmond sat in Morris the Magician's special chair and waited, while his mum talked to Morris outside. He was trying to be brave and fearless, as he knew a good dragon should be, but his knees kept knocking together at the thought of what Morris might do. Then Morris came in and sat on a stool next to him and asked Desmond to open his mouth wide.

"This won't hurt," he said.

"Uh, huh, uh, huh, mmm," muttered Morris. "Ah yes, yes, I have it, I can see the problem." He smiled at Desmond. "You have a bone caught behind one of your fangs and it's pressing into the gum. The bone is stuck quite fast which is why your fang brush couldn't get it out. You do brush your fangs, don't you, Desmond?" asked Morris, sternly.

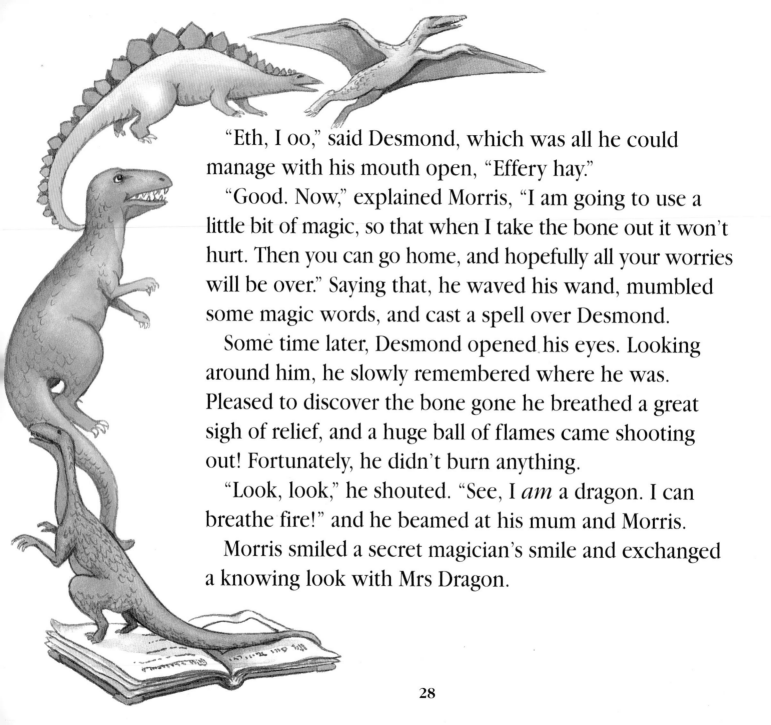

"Eth, I oo," said Desmond, which was all he could manage with his mouth open, "Effery hay."

"Good. Now," explained Morris, "I am going to use a little bit of magic, so that when I take the bone out it won't hurt. Then you can go home, and hopefully all your worries will be over." Saying that, he waved his wand, mumbled some magic words, and cast a spell over Desmond.

Some time later, Desmond opened his eyes. Looking around him, he slowly remembered where he was. Pleased to discover the bone gone he breathed a great sigh of relief, and a huge ball of flames came shooting out! Fortunately, he didn't burn anything.

"Look, look," he shouted. "See, I *am* a dragon. I can breathe fire!" and he beamed at his mum and Morris.

Morris smiled a secret magician's smile and exchanged a knowing look with Mrs Dragon.

"Of course you can," he said. "We always knew you would when the time was right. You can't hurry these things you know. I think you will find that you can unfold your wings now as well."

Desmond looked at Morris mystified.

Mrs Dragon thanked the magician and she and Desmond went outside. Then, without thinking, Desmond unfurled his tightly folded wings — they had been there all along. He nearly fell over with surprise. Desmond's mum smiled.

"I think you're ready to try flying now. Perhaps we can practice on the way home."

Excitedly, Desmond waved goodbye to Morris, who, still smiling a secret magician's smile, was watching from his cave window.

Desmond opened his wings and wobbled into the air.

Then, his confidence growing, he soared up into the sky and flew round a few times — looking and feeling like the noble dragon he was.

And finally, he flew home for tea with his mum.